P9-CQF-762

I'm Big!

by **Milton Schafer** * pictures by **Joanne Lew-Vriethoff**

Dial Books for **Young Readers**

To Cecile Goyette, who is wise to the word, discriminating in counsel, and
a model of encouragement, my humble thanks for being Bigger and Better
—M.S.

To my parents, Maarten, Dwight, Tristan, Anaïs, and my beautiful Max
—J.L.V.

DIAL BOOKS FOR YOUNG READERS • A division of Penguin Young Readers Group • Published by The Penguin Group • Penguin Group (USA) Inc., 375 Hudson Street, New York, NY 10014, U.S.A. • Penguin Group (Canada), 90 Eglinton Avenue East, Suite 700, Toronto, Ontario, Canada M4P 2Y3 (a division of Pearson Penguin Canada Inc.) • Penguin Books Ltd, 80 Strand, London WC2R 0RL, England • Penguin Ireland, 25 St. Stephen's Green, Dublin 2, Ireland (a division of Penguin Books Ltd) • Penguin Books India Pvt Ltd, 11 Community Centre, Panchsheel Park, New Delhi - 110 017, India • Penguin Group (NZ), Cnr Airborne and Rosedale Roads, Albany, Auckland, New Zealand (a division of Pearson New Zealand Ltd) • Penguin Books (South Africa) (Pty) Ltd, 24 Sturdee Avenue, Rosebank, Johannesburg 2196, South Africa • Penguin Books Ltd, Registered Offices: 80 Strand, London WC2R 0RL, England • Text copyright © 2006 by Milton Schafer and Michael Zager • Pictures copyright © 2006 by Joanne Lew-Vriethoff • All rights reserved • The publisher does not have any control over and does not assume any responsibility for author or third-party websites or their content. • Designed by Lily Malcom and Joanne Lew-Vriethoff • Text set in Imperfect Bold • Manufactured in China on acid-free paper • Library of Congress Cataloging-in-Publication Data • Schafer, Milton. I'm big! / by Milton Schafer ; pictures by Joanne Lew-Vriethoff. • p. cm. • Summary: A boy relates all the things he can do now that he is big. • ISBN 0-8037-3022-5 • [1. Size—Fiction. 2. Growth—Fiction. 3. Self-confidence—Fiction. 4. Stories in rhyme.] I. Lew-Vriethoff, Joanne, ill. II. Title. • PZ8.3.S2893Im 2006 • [E]—dc22 • 2004019409 • 10 9 8 7 6 5 4 3 2 1

The art was created from ink line drawings and completed in Adobe Photoshop.

I can dress myself,

I don't need Mom to help me anymore.

And when I sit in my father's chair, my feet can reach the floor—

see that?

I'm **big!**

I'm big!

Got a muscle and I'm big.

When I wrestle with my cousin Jill,

in a **second** she's on the ground,

so **Nutso** and **Red** better not get wise,

'cause I don't fool around.

I can throw this rock a mile away
and bean that rattlesnake.

Ya dare me to swallow my

chewing gum

and **not** get a

bellyache?

When I was in the jungle

I frightened all the **animals**,

and even Tarzan ran a mile

when I was **King** of the **Cannibals!**

I lived there for about . . .

ten years . . .

And then a **big ship** found me . . .

When I got back, first thing you know

the **COPS** were all around me.

They started buggin' me with questions,

I clammed right up and took the heat.

Then I turned my back and walked away,

right across the street.

I'm
allowed!

'Course once I was small,

but now . . .

You see that fence about

ten feet high?

I can jump it—

backwards too!

I fed a **lion** a hot dog once
when I was at the zoo.
(They let me in the cage—**no problem!**)

I can climb a mountain blindfolded

with a forty-five-pound pack,

And paddle down a river

on an alligator's back.

I can look a camel in the eye
and never even

blink.

In gym I lift a **hundred pounds.**

I'm way bigger than you think.

I'm big!
I'm **big!**
I'm a big kid now!

I'm big!

My mother doesn't yell at me
just for going without a hat.
She knows darn well I'd run away,
because I'm **too old** for that!

What does she think, I'm a baby?

No way!

What does she think,

I'm a shrimp?

Go 'way!

You oughtta see me

ride a crazy horse,

and drive my father's car,

of course.

I'm **big!** I'm big!

So big, I'm major league.

I'm even bigger than big,

I'm MAJOR *b-e-e-e-e-g!*

I mean . . .

I'm big . . . but not **THAT** big.

I'm only a little big.

But you know what?

So what if it's a monster?

I can handle that.

I'll tackle him behind his back

and stuff him in my sack.

You dare me?

He don't scare me.

You know why?

'Cause I'm big.

I'm **super-
duper-galooper
big!**